I0615191

Rollo Russell

Break of day and other poems

Rollo Russell

Break of day and other poems

ISBN/EAN: 9783744722773

Printed in Europe, USA, Canada, Australia, Japan

Cover: Foto ©Andreas Hilbeck / pixelio.de

More available books at **www.hansebooks.com**

AND OTHER POEMS

BY

ROLLO RUSSELL

London

T. FISHER UNWIN

PATERNOSTER SQUARE

MDCCCXCIII

CONTENTS.

TRANSLATIONS.

ORISONS AND HYMNS.

TO THE SPIRIT OF WISDOM.

IN THE WORLD-CATHEDRAL.

O Word of God writ in the life of worlds,
Kind influence flowing from the far All Good,
Spring of unseen and everlasting light,
In which the spirits of the just go forth
And have their being ; ever-present Sun
Hidden awhile like this material star
By earth and clouds, yet shining without pause
Within the orbit of each human heart,
Spirit of Wisdom, whose pale broken beams,
Through man's dark sorrows struggling, reach
    their end
Alight as to their haven in true minds,
Beating soul-music on our clay-bound life,
The praise hymn of high heaven faintly
    caught,
Tidings of that new world where all un-
    marred
The law of God works out the consort full,
Help us, O Spirit, to receive Thy gift
As worthy, and as knowing but in part,
Most humble, because most aware of Thee ;

Not in the pride of knowledge hardly won,
Nor scornful of the foolish wandering steps
Which might have been our own, but un-
   abashed,
Praising the Giver of so much new light
As our own vain spirits may with reverence
   bear.
Come wisdom, silent new-creating joy,
That habitest the temple of pure hearts,
Eternal treasure of the angel host,
Yielding unmeasured hope not matched with
   sense
That gazes wonderstruck through Time's
   harsh night,—
Thou seest further than mere numbers teach,
Beyond the stars, beyond this paltry stage ;
Not most in matter, nor obedient globes,
Nor things nor energy that blindly move,
Though these be great, is thy quest satisfied,
But in the contrite God-adoring love,
Faithful through doubt, unquenched through
   seas of flame—
Working, responsive to the heavenly will,
The highest good, the service most divine,
The hidden glory of the great Unknown,
Whence a new nobleness makes perfect life.

INFANCY.

A CRY from out the unknown vasty void,
A life new come to this dim shadowy stage,
· A spiritual graft put forth from Heaven.
A fresh-formed wavelet on the sea of pain,
Woke by the gentle touch of morning air
To droop or grow, speeding we know not
    where,
A poor weak wavelet on the boundless main.
A faint far cry that feels no listener near,
Pale vacant wonder without hope or fear,
Gazing bewildered on the moving scene ;
No time, no space, now seeking what things
    mean,
Anon in dreamless sleep reseeking night,
Now claiming in loud untaught tones the
    right
Of helpless instinct to be helped to live.
O strange and piteous sight, wan hope of
    man,
Most venerable portent, but in form
Contemptible beyond all earthly things,
Bearing no mark of a divine descent,
No presage of the glory of mankind !

The chick that hops forth from its prisoning
    shell,
Strides the green planet with more jaunty
    wit
Than thou, soft crumb of ugly mottled flesh
By twenty months informed.   This is our
    pride,
That thou art most removed from competence,
Least nature-favoured because least her child.
Wailest thou, little one, from thy blank heart,
Unconscious witness to the imperfect world ?
Or is it but the stirring of life-force
Around thy inner self—not thee, but for thee
Demanding that by which the budding germ,
Not of the flesh, may be retained, held fast,
And gather strength within the strengthening
    house
Here in our low arena of decay,
Where the fair springtime scatters killing
    frosts,
And flowers and ashes mingle at our feet,
Cause ever chasing cause ?   Or is that cry
So heart-constraining, woful-powerful,
The mere crude working of chance heat and
    sound
Playing the truant in a baby's throat ?
How grates it then so keenly on stern souls ?
Has dull gross matter made this pact with
    force :—
To build a toy called living, which shall be

Precious to hearts which can survey the
    world
And bend their passions to the will of God ?
O monstrous learning, mining down to hell,
Rise to the light ere darkness quench thine
    eye,
And let the sun be ever sun to thee,
Nor ask, self-buried 'neath the ponderous rocks,
Whether indeed he be so fair and strong,
Or whether some deep-pent volcanic fire
Nourish the health of the bright fields above
Rather than he. What Hercules of thought
Can pile the godlike on material things,
And crown new Order of old protean Chaos
With praise for Mind from Matter well
    evolved ?
We speak of incommensurable things—
Unfeeling matter driven by nerveless force—
As windmills by the wind, and lo ! a thing
Sentient, beloved, harping our soul's chords,
Subject to powers of higher ancestry
And ruling kingdoms of ethereal love ;
A motive power, the fixed human will,
To which all storms that vex the Arctic seas,
Or thundering falls of Californian alps,
Or centuries of sunshine through all space
Bear no proportion. Enough, mute angel,
May'st thou ne'er wander thus in troublous
    thought,
But peace be with thee, 'spite an age of strife

As in the downy crib, so calm through life.
So calm ! yet looking on thy deep repose
Like flower with petals closed unwittingly,
The murmur of the piping world not heard
Even in the echo of dream-music,
My wish returns to me, it cannot be
That in the clash and shock of mightier wars
Than ever nation against nation waged
All blessing can lie in tranquillity.
Earth is a battlefield for heaven and hell,
Heart against heart, the civil war of souls,
The fermentation which shall leave things
    clear,
The long death-grapple wherein one must
    fall,
Evil or good, this I must rather wish,
Since he who strives not is accounted dead,
And all who choose may fight as sons of God.
Weapons are given, and the time to strike.
Then, like a hero, fraught with Heaven's
    command,
Thine eye firm-set on incorruptible ends,
With strength surmounting wave on wave of
    woe,
With patient service and delivering wrath,
Perfect in love, unclaimed by Time or Death,
Thou shalt know victory where God is all.

YOUTH.

I.

L<small>IFTING</small> of hearts in the joy of the morning,
Bright hope and bravery, trusting and scorn-
    ing,
Visions of beauty, delectable mountains,
Sparkling of dewdrops and fresh-springing
    fountains ;
Eagles, the beat of whose vanes, as they soar
In the throb of the sunburst, spurns the low
    shore,
Plumage of silver and broad wings resplen-
    dent,
Circling and wheeling and motionless pendent,
Eyes, that undazzled, triumphantly gleaming,
Flash the proud presage of daring and
    dreaming ;—
Breaking of chains from the limbs of the
    right,
Melting of wrong in the sea of God's light,
Tremblers made bold in the might of the free,
Realms of fair wisdom to every degree,
Every man prince of the nobles of thought

Garnering harvests where prophets have
    wrought ;
Kingly beneficence, large as man's story,
Calling new worlds to the kinship of glory ;
Clear-shining honour, glad-glittering for battle,
Lightnings whose thunders o'er nations loud
    rattle ;
Passion for homes earned by slain warrior
    sires,
Swift swords of truth dipt in martyrs pure
    fires,
Charging and clashing of steel in the sun,
Grappling of axes till standards are won ;—
Bearing o'er oceans the flag of reform,
Plowing alone through the heart of the
    storm ;
Islands released from the grasp of the deep,
Continents thrilling and waking from sleep,
Voices and songs of humanity sounding,
Liberty, peace, and fraternity founding,
Anthems of labour, and servitude choral,
Poesy flashing in streamers auroral,
Touching the beacons from summit to summit,
Crossing great waters unsounded by plummet,
Firing the torch of a world-wide crusade,
Peoples in counsel for every man's aid,
Banners dyed new in the candour of Christ,
Lances of force in salvation baptised ;—
Flowers and fruit of the garden of praise,
Rivers of melody, bowers of grace,

Sweet-breathing meadows o'erbrimming the
 lake,
Choirs in the branches and song in the brake,
Gentle enchantment and mellowing care,
Waving of wings as if angels were there,
Growing tranquillity, loveliness, rest,
Setting of sails for the land of the blest.

So softly dreaming of a heavenly world,
All life lay sensitive in conscious sleep,
Breathing deep wisdom of pure melody,—
Celestial music pealing from the spheres
Eternal harmonics, which, as they move,
Give calm unto the soul, a sea of sound
Full-fraught with worship joining man to God.

II.

Behold! behold! it is no mortal power
Speeding like light for ever through the
 spheres,
While this mere sun of days and time sinks
 lower,
On human orbs the ray divine appears.
Long have we crept by shattered groves and
 thrones,
Long have we hoped where cause for hope
 had fled,
Oft have we mingled unavailing groans,
Deep have we searched among the famous dead;

Their time is past, the ages know their own ;
We cannot build upon the tombs of seers,
Words writ in sand we may not grave in stone,
Nor raise the corpses of forgotten fears.
All that our hearts need bear—behold within !
The ghosts of centuries yet haunt our souls,
We view the heights of Truth and wilds of
    Sin,
Ours the great Now which all to come controls.
Let us then rise with spirits full and free
And cast the crust of custom's mould away,—
We are the ministers of worlds to be,
We are possessors of a waneless day.
For weal or woe, the truth must be our care,
Through depth and height, the truth must be
    our cry,
For truth, all dangers we must gladly dare,
Live for her glory, and be proud to die.
Where is the faith more noble, strong,
    supreme,
To lift our souls beyond the ills of Time,
Than that which, darksome though the pas-
    sage seem,
Believes the Heart of Knowledge Good Sub-
    lime ?
So may the tempest roar, the sun grow dark,
And trackless vapours hide our guiding star ;
As from a thundercloud the hymning lark,
Our dauntless voices shall be heard afar.
And as this planet and our sun of light,

The dust of firmaments we know and see,
And all the vaster spheres beyond our sight
Revolve around the Central World to be,
So may our spirits, through the chasm of night,
Swayed by heaven's love be never prone to
    fall,
Cheered by each small true beam of starry
    light
Obey the influence of the God of All.
For shall the monarch of creation quail
At every step and crush his noblest power,
Shall Nature's fables o'er the soul prevail,
And Virtue weave herself a Hadian bower?
Shall we, safe-havened from the jostling
    world,
Where songs divine so chafed with common
    noise,
Kneel the sad night out with our banner
    furled,
And mock the Godhead with man-pleasing
    toys?
Wilt thou, poor bird, that beat'st the nether
    air
And view'st with fear the conquests of this
    age,
Yield thy frail freedom to some good man's
    care
And coax warm comfort from thy narrow
    cage?
If such thy lot, farewell and take thine ease,

For glorious war is stirring in our hearts,
The war of worlds, the war of God for man,
The war of Love against the powers of Hate,
Darkness of soul and arsenals of night,—
While these oppose, in this corporeal life,
Action is happiness, and peace unrest ;
And neither death nor principalities,
Nor schemers of the treason of the world,
Nor priests of the anathemas of hell,
Nor false interpreters of God's high will
Above the nations by their Mammon throned,
Nor whispering charms of pharisaic lips,
Warning the faithful to avert their eyes,
And banish Reason from hand-hallowed heads,
Nor all the anti-christs with Christian lips,
Nor planished heathendom with church and
     creed,
Nor blinding peaks of philosophic ice,
Nor depth, nor height, nor might, nor multi-
     tude,
Shall ever sunder us from love of truth,
Or ever make us doubt the truth of love.

III.

Praise be to God for His first glorious gift
Of life, and living a true life to Him,
Born to the freedom of the heirs of heaven,
As earth, yet spirit, mortal, without death,
Joyful in strength and glad in the pure beams

Long time invisible to keener sight
That stretch a pathway for the soul's long
    flight
Across all ages through the star-sown deep,
When her set work on earth's green fields is
    done,
And willing labour yields to willing sleep.
O rapturous contest with the stubborn world!
O happy vision of victorious strife!
Beneath the arching blue of God's bright sky
No heart shall faint, no comrade sheath his
    sword,
For if the Lord of Hosts be on our side
Surely a mighty task with might is done,
Strong walls smoke up in powder at the Voice
The sounding of the angel's trumpet call,
The glad heroic blast of conquering faith
Proclaiming peace in every groaning land,
Truth-seeking freedom and divinest love,
The great religion melting sect and creed,
The new-won heritage of unity,
The will of God on earth as done in heaven.
    Fall, fall, ye forts where blighting envy
        broods
    And hollow pride, and timorous Folly's
        crew,
    Hushing high thought, and jingling keys to
        heaven,
    Bear record and dissolve in burning words,
    Bear record and be witnesses for ever ;—

Within each heart our Father's kingdom is!
Then may fair humbleness with contrite
feet
Do justice and love mercy day by day,
And murmur not, but ever watch and pray
That we may know and knowing keep the
way.
So all day long a melody goes forth
From hearts responsive to ethereal tones
Straight-lighted from their everlasting home,
Where songs more lovely than poor strings
and wind
Can dare to emulate on this low world
Resound unfading multitudinous praise
With deathless music, of which some pale
notes
Come to the straining heart not through the
ear,
And fill the unclosed expanse from sphere
to sphere.

IV.

How can I tell with struggling tale, O Love,
Launched far beyond the shores of time and
space
In flight beyond the empyrean blue,
A mind that hath no utterance of words
Or cognisance of creeping sentences ;—
The Universe of Life could not proclaim,

Though every being in one chorus joined
And not one letter of their story strayed,
Nor can all eloquence of human kind
Translate a sentence of the heart of song
That lives its own life in the great Unseen.
The sad world breaks her gloom with words of
    light,
Surely she blossometh in new-found joy,
Winter is dying from the hearts of men,
Nature confessing putteth off her sins,
And blesseth heaven with divine discourse ;
God's world, ourselves, made pure and void
    of fear,
Full of repentance which cannot repent,
Grow perfect in the rapture of release :
An air of music borne on pinions bright
Breathes heaven through me, and my whole
    soul melts
In floods of glory compassing all space ;
I am at one with every star that shines,
And grain of sand and drop of diamond dew ;
Streams are for tears of joy and hills for
    smiles,
And earth's fair tapestry my silent speech,—
The perfect concord of a thousand thoughts
Uncalled, unlaboured, rendering sweet praise
So various, and so full of high intent
And love and grace beholding life indeed,
That nothing can endure in such pure light
But only good and everlasting right.

Yet were this poor earth painless we should
  fall
Into the windless peril of still seas,
Placid bright waters of forgetfulness,
Because the might of care which could not
  suffer
Some deep apocalypse of pain and proof
Would range for sacrifice beyond the grave,
To find eternity, or droop in dreams.
But thou hast made my woful life complete,
And thou hast armed me for a thousand
  toils,
And thou hast sealed my fitful doubting
  soul,
And thou hast come to crown my nobler
  hours,
And hidden honour finds full joy in thee,
And all the ends of action meet in thee,
And thou hast saved me from the elements
That beat about the dim coasts of the
  known,
Not earthly, and hast taught me to behold
The grace of God that passeth every art,
The Reason that for ever moves in love.
Love hath no limits laid in time and space,
Nor corporal bands, nor fear of earth's vast
  woes,
Her home is with the universal light,
Joy lifts her wings and cleaves her crystal
  way,

And every breath against her feeds her
   flight ;
Nought is too small for her and nought too
   great
For boundless pity and immense delight ;
Heaven flows through all and common
   grows divine,
Rays not for time through menial moments
   shine,
Strong for all fates, to death itself supreme,
Life makes her but a visit and departs a
   dream.

A MAY MORNING.

O who that has plunged in the crystal stream
When the sun's in the gate of the golden East,
Who feels the light airs around him play
With quickening breath while the beams of
    day
Encrimson the court of the clouds that wait,
And dewy leaves shake their sparkling
    freight,
And the hosts of the living to gladness wake,
And the lark his carol of praise doth make,
And the mavis pours forth his roundelay,
And the gentle doves murmur the tale of
    May,
And the fresh flowers lift their bent-down
    eyes
To look up in love on the blue, blue skies,
When the world seems born for eternal youth
And to sing of joy and mercy and truth,
When the moaning of sadness has trembled to
    rest,
And the great sea heaves with a tender breast,
And colours break forth in rainbow tints
From the gossamered meadows and hardest
    flints,

All drinking, scattering, telling of light
Which cometh from heaven, for heaven is
    bright ;
O who can despair, in so sweet an air,
And doubt that the image of truth is fair ?

A VISION OF THE WORLD'S PROGRESS.

I SAW the nations marching on,
    Marching to the bounds of time,
They were one in heart and purpose,
    Mighty in their golden prime.

Lo! the world's long wilful childhood,
    Yielding to maturer thought,
One united federation,
    Truth and endless wisdom sought.

Nobly shone this Christian army,
    Full of strength and void of doubt,
Voices of all lands in union
    Raised the same triumphant shout.

Dangers fell as if by magic
    At the stroke of faith so great,
Rivers parted, mountains vanished,
    Hurtful creatures met their fate.

Countless banners of the legions
    Waved them onward in their course,
Each man bore his crest peculiar,
    And, above, the Holy Cross.

Mild and gentle was their bearing,
    For no earthly foe was near,
Watchful, clad in heavenly armour,
    Thus they had no fiend to fear.

It was morning when I saw them,
    As they marched they sang this song :
It was evening when I saw them,
    As they marched they sang this song :

Forward for truth, forward for knowledge,
    Forward for mercy and love ;
O Thou whom we daily acknowledge,
    Lighten our ways from above !
Keep us Thine own, our senses are weak,
    Lift them from earthly deceit,
Quicken slow hearts Thy kingdom to seek,
    Strengthen the zeal of our feet !
Forward for truth, forward for knowledge,
    Forward in mercy and love ;
O Thou whom we daily acknowledge,
    Glory ! descend from above.

RENENS-SUR-ROCHE.

PERCHED on thy rocky nest,
    Leafy retreat,
Be thou the traveller's rest,
    Welcome and sweet.
When from the busy din,
    Dusty and worn,
He thy fair heights doth win,
    Care lags forlorn.
Ne'er let her climb that steep,
    Drop her at last ;
There let her weep and sleep,
    Witch of the past.
Once on that happy hill
    Every man's free ;
Fixed by no narrow will
    Fool's fashions flee.
Here the great mountains preach
    Joy in repose,
Field, lake, and forest teach
    More than our prose.

1871.

BREAK OF DAY.

A SKYLARK'S TRILL.

UPSPRINGING silently, outringing fervently,
Shaking the dew of the dark from my wings,
Up to the glowing sky, up to the heavens
    high,
World-filling fountain of fathomless light !

Praise for the dawning gray, praise for the
    morning ray,
Praise for the fill of content in my breast,
Air of the firmament speckless in purity,
Crystal ethereal ocean of light !

Beams of the crimson East, touch with your
    fire the least,
Make me a worshipper filled with your might ;
Sun ! make one meeting thee raptured in
    greeting thee,
Angel impassioned of starry delight !

Poising invisible, free in sublimity,
Din of toil drowned in a carol of joy,
Shadow turned shining, for love hath in-
    spirited,
Faith through her winter wrought sorrow to
    song !

Over the kindly earth, over the waving trees,
Over the groves and the harbours of rest,
Flowers unnumbered outbidding my trustful-
    ness,
Sweetness and beauty enshrining my nest !

Freshness of forest and bloom of the wilder-
    ness,
Rippling of rivers and smiles of the sea,
Flock-dappled hillocks and dells of forgetful-
    ness,
Boons brimming over the heart of the free !

Keen through the fanning wind soaring
    hilariously,
Swift will I rally and mount to the blue,
Down for a moment to sally tumultuously,
Braving with pæans the welkin anew !

Dome of broad ecstasy, holy immensity,
Measureless, measureless, bounty of light,
Flame-hidden potency, primal intensity !
Sphering with music the gladness of flight !

Join with me, join with me, spirits illuminate,
Praise with me, praise with me, wingless and
    wise,
Blithe be your melody's yearning felicity,
Fill your deep vision from infinite skies !

Quitting the virid earth, kindle in vivid mirth,
Glitter aloft a wild torrent of glee,
Burst from infirmity, plunge in eternity,
Lowly and gentle alight on the lea !

AD ALMAM.

THINE eyes are like the arch above,
   A depth of clearness, heavenly light ;
A depth which as we wonder grows
   More darkly blue, serenely bright.

Thy blush is like the softest cloud
   Set glowing in the pearly west,
Sure token of a sunny heart,
   That beats to make our being blest.

Thy steadfast mien of high intent
   Ennobles looks that meet thy face,
And lives unconsciously are blent
   With something of thy winsome grace.

ON AN OLD TOMBSTONE.

THROUGH the dark gateway into life and light
The body fallen, the spirit pure and free,
Pains raised in joy and wrongs of earth made
    right,
And faith that wept made perfectly to see.
O may Thy children who still struggle here
Rejoice in God and live for Him alone,
Work be our prayer, and love bereft of fear,
Our truest worship His will known and done.

UBI DIES ?

THE light is gone, but not from heaven,
 Though night close on our eyes,
The beams of day to earth once given
 Still travel through the skies.

Our life is dark, the soul's hid sun
 Shall wake our song no more ;
Have other worlds the message won
 Which gladdened this wild shore ?

ALETHEIA.

THY smile illuminates the day,
My weight of care thy voice doth ease,
Thy tender help doth smoothe my way,
And all thy words and counsels please.

Thou art to me a better heart,
Clouds clear and show me sky above,
New powers into being start
Beneath the blessing of thy love.

So mortal may in mortal rest,
And work from heaven all his days,
And even griefs that rend his breast
Sow music for immortal praise.

TO MY MOTHER.

WHEN skies are bright and spring is kind,
When sunset glories hold the mind,
When flowers wear their sweetest air
And leafy woodland waves most fair,
      Then thou art near.

When books most please, both old and new,
When speech is apt and wit is true,
When art and science lift our seeing
To regions of diviner being,
      Thou art not far.

When winter days like May are bright,
When stars impress the silent night,
When hope, though oft cast down, believes,
When strength through dark distress achieves,
      Thought turns to thee.

A quiet garden next the mart,—
A hymn heard in the city's heart,—
Amid the throng a voice of rest
Inspiring war to win the best,—
      The tones are thine.

TO N.

THE skylark singing loud and clear
From dawn to dusk for all to hear,
The nightingale, with glorious pleading,
Through rain and thunder nothing heeding,
The bluebells bending dewy heads,
The may that now her snow-wreath sheds,
The dappled show of flower and tree
So fragrant, generous, and free ;—
All these must make a present poor,
So I leave nothing at your door,
But only say,—To each glad thing,
When winter comes, be thou like spring.

HUNTING SONG.

See the morning is adorning all with golden
    sunny light ;
There's no scorning such a warning for whom
    hunting is delight.
Sol is gaining, Luna waning, and the stars
    have shut their eyes ;
Last night's feigning to be raining with the
    gray night quickly flies ;
There's a twittering and a tittering of birdlings
    just awake,
Don't be frittering time while glittering shine
    the wavelets on the lake ;
Prick with bright spurs to the green furze
    whence old Reynard bolts away ;
Brook no demurs when your blood stirs at the
    breaking of the day.
Your noble steed can hardly feed, he's all
    trembling for the chase ;
With boldest deed he'll serve thy need in the
    hottest of the race.
Then forward hark, as blithe as lark, to the
    meeting on the slope,
Where the glad bark in the grand park is a
    greeting full of hope.

VIOLA.

O violet, sweetest of flowers, dear gift of a
    loving Creator,
Why dost thou lower thy head, and hide in
    thy dewy green leaflets ?
Long hath my spirit sought thee, and would
    almost have perished without thee,
Heaven's meek token of faith, low angel to
    desolate sadness,
Breathing mercy and peace, and mildly winning
    to gladness,
Gently reproving our rage and bidding us
    hearken to conscience,
Turning the stubborn thought back, replacing
    the good for amendment.
Spring is the season of joy and of blossom and
    opening leaf-buds,
Then more warmly the sun, more tenderly
    shineth the moon-beam ;
Daintily capers the fawn, gaily the lamb in the
    meadow,
Yet my heart hath been hard, unmoved by
    repentance around it ;

Struck by the waves of new life, no echo came
    gladly responsive,
Shrouded by grief in a tomb, swooning away
    in despair,
But thou hast come like the touch of the note
    that alone could awake me.
Now there shall dwell in my soul a hymn of
    lowly contentment.

GENOA.

PROUD city of the azure gulf!
  Who said thou wast no more?
Who sailing on thy furrowed bay
  Saw ruin on thy shore?

The days of thy magnificence
  Were all too bright to last;
A cloud has overshadowed thee,
  But it will soon be past!

Superbly stand thy palaces,
  Still dost thou climb the steep,
Aspiring to the snowy Alps,
  And sprinkled o'er the deep.

And east and west thy glory spreads
  In crescent-like array,
And far beyond on either side
  Soft shines the olive gray.

Great Italy shall live again
  More nobly than of yore;
And wilt thou lag in slow decay
  Forgetting all before?

Rise, Genoa ! and Venice, rise !
   Pillars of art and fame ;
When you excel she leads the world ;
   Your torpor is her shame.

Then enterprise and courage come,
   And languid ease depart !
All hardy virtues help thee on,
   And flourish in thy heart !

1871.

THE DEATH OF SOCRATES.

BY ONE WHO HEARD HIM.

GONE! he is gone, the master whom we loved,
We know not whither, but we know 'tis well;
He grieved not for the parting of his soul
From the poor frame; therefore we must not
     grieve;
Two angels led him, Memory and Hope,
Childlike and shining through the gate of
     death,
Unruffled by resentment or dismay;
Feeling the breath of a more glorious day
Upon his brows, his burden fell away.

Weep not that he is gone; 'tis better now
In honour and in strength, since death must
     come,
Than that with overburdened weight of years
A flagging body should offend that mind
So deep, so passionate, so true.   No time

Can kill what he has left, mountains of
    thought,
And pleasant lands where future men may
    roam
Untired in exploit, spreading far and wide,
Making their homes where desert once dis-
    mayed.
How that one life enriched an idle world!
How that one death ennobled it! My friends,
Let us think of him as philosophers
And his disciples, of that soul with joy,
Which looked with joy upon the highest
    things,
Though hidden far from common sense and
    touch
Beyond all mortal ken, we know not why.
No little troubles vexed him in his walk,
No superstitious vanities annoyed.
His trouble was the error of his kind,
His highest care to find and teach the truth.
If all were like him, we should all be free,
By crime unharrowed, undistrest by pain,
And, bearing natural evil with a smile,
Secure that what our Deity offends
In earthy substance, cannot live hereafter,
Nor bind the spirit still with envious chains,
Nor make this muddy cast, this floating isle,
More than a guest-house for what came from
    God.
Brethren, our Master has bequeathed us more

Than ever man was heir to, the bequest
To make right known and to exalt our kind
In spite of what the world may do or say,
The privilege to die, if death be good,
The dignity of hate, if hate be wrong,
The perfect bond of love for evermore.

THE SCEPTIC.

HE stands alone like some sea-sundered rock,
Which all the seething surge around defies,
Looking upon the cliffs to which it once was
    joined,
And grieving o'er the mighty swept away.
Gravely he sorrows for the vacant space,
But never bows his head, for he must stand
And bear the flowing years which lesser
    strength
Declined, and trembled and for ever sank.
So firm, so sad, so scornful, and so true,
The sceptic looks upon his fellows dear
Across the mournful waste of moaning brine,
And hopes for naught and gives the past a
    sigh.
There was a time when all was fresh and gay,
When he would fall upon his knees in tears
And lift on high the praises of his heart
With inward peace, and hold divine discourse.
Too noble to make wrong, he spurns the false ;
His mighty mind works groping towards the
    truth ;

His deep humility proclaims no faith,
But one within in silence counsels him.
O blame him not, assailed by every foe,
And blasted in the midst of his bright life,
If now no comfort can enfold his age ;
Bear with him lovingly, for still he loves.

THE AGNOSTIC.

THOU know'st no God, thou can'st not find
    the Sun ;
Since night is true, to thee there is no day ;
Blind to thee blind the strife of good and ill,
Time but a segment of the wheel of fate,
The world an accident of shadowy space,
Man born to learn that all must be unlearnt,
And, knowledge wanting, faith and reason
    vain.
Behold the changeless law o'er all supreme,—
Who made the law that works to higher ends ?
Behold the tender grace of star and flower,—
Who made thee conscious of their softening
    power ?
Behold the snowflake exquisite in form,—
Was it made perfect by unwilling norm ?
Behold thy senses, mind, and heart,—
Is there no purpose in thy conscious soul ?
And canst thou make thy ignorance thy god ?
Duty is not the breath of cloudy dreams ;
Love is not matter struck by senseless force ;

Force has not contemplation in itself,
The world of spirit is above the seen,
And in the spirit dwells the Life of life.
Leave then thy load upon the miry ways,
And plant thy garden on the hill of praise.
There breathe beyond the cold fume-shrouded
    plain,
And make thy desert land to bloom again.

PREPARATION.

How gloriously the day comes after night !
How spring excels the level summer time !
How are we honoured by adversity !
Now God's love like the dawn by contrast
    speaks
And wins the eye that comprehended not.
We are not made for lifelong happiness
To hold this world a little paradise,
And mere contentment as our being's end,
Or to be great without much agony.
The plough must pass across the tender sense ;
Frost, heat, and winnowing must prepare the
    grain ;
The Bread of Life was made our joy by pain

THE REVOLUTIONARY IDEALIST BEFORE EXECUTION.

PARIS, 1871.

AND if I die, my soul shall spurn the tomb
And robe herself for battle once again,
To finish where the poor weak flesh has failed,
Not with the sinews of this groping arm
But strong in death my spirit shall arise,
And, purified by visions hid from earth,
Shall sound the war-song of a nobler race,
Who, like their fathers on this mighty day,
Fear not to break through custom's leaden
    chains ;
And every heart that bound itself in life
To march in van of our eternal cause
Shall live again upon another field ;
And O may that be bloodless ! may we breathe
A gentle blessing on a willing age !
May not the luxury and wealth of one
Drawn from the well-springs of a thousand
    homes,
The curse of poverty, the tares of ease,
The choking fungus and ill-weeds of gain,

The bitter treason of despotic rule,
The preference of ruin to repair,
And of repair to building all afresh,
Then be the will and pleasure of mankind.
That time is very far, but it will come,
And we have erred in catching at the fruit
Before the flower has dropt ; but it will come,
For when they break oppression's flinty husk,
And know the bounty of the equal boon,
Then will they thank us that we found the
    tree
And planted it for future happiness.
Yes, thou great Future, bear me witness now
That we poor fools who build among the clouds
Shall not descend while they approach the sun,
But shine the brighter for the foil of night
When they look back upon dark history.
We have done wrong, most shameful grievous
    wrong,
In running to rebellion.   O the pang
We suffered silently, when we had made
The channels that should water all the land,
And on a sudden saw them overflowed
By muddy torrents gathered in the hills,
Sweeping away our labour and our care.
It was a thrilling moment of despair,
Counsel and thought fled scared before the
    flood,
And some were lifted by it and became its
    tools.

We should have stood against it, but the brain,
Raptured, unmoored, delirious to behold
The passion cherished as its own possess
The stormy current of a frantic crowd,
Welcomes the whirlwind, sanctifies its rage,
And rides exultant on the foaming wave.
Most heavy anguish settled on our hearts
When through the ruin horrid vices loomed
And dashed Hope's image from our happy
    dreams.
Then every rogue, professing common good,
Worked out his crooked profitable way,
And great reforms, which should have come
    like spring,
To ope the budding virtues of our land,
Were marred by plagues of fattened selfishness
More fatal than the Eastern locust-swarm,
Which sucks the sap and blackens all the fields.
Still I have faith, for through the soul of each
Strife shall prepare for Nature's home-coming
Each man must raise himself to smite the fiend
Which in himself, as in the rich and proud,
Works common evil, and the Golden Age
Must reign in hearts before it fashions life.
My fate is fallen, I must pass away ;
Work-days are short, eternity is long,
May all good fare with you to endless joy.

ON SEEING A LETTER SIGNED "JANE THE QUEEN," AT LOSELY, IN SURREY.

DEAR type of good on earth's rude stage,
  Wise, gentle " Jane the Queen " !
How hadst thou blest that ruffian age !
  What healing might have been !

Thy soaring spirit walled in stone,
  Thy loving heart beat down,
Books, truest friends, kept faith alone,
  The rest but served a crown.

So, in this world, confusion's might
  Gives ten days' reign to grace ;
And when glad eyes first welcome light,
  Death runs to take her place.

August, 1885.

MIGHTY WORKS.

There are no miracles, nor ever were,
　So must we learn, and faint with pain ;
Yet so we grow to higher prayer,
　And weakness turns to truer gain.

All, all are miracles ; each day and hour
　We move in mysteries profound,
Each leaf and flower is work of power,
　And every inch is hallowed ground.

The passing sunbeam doth surpass all story,
　Each drop of dew is eloquent,
Through common things we see a world of
　　glory,
　And law makes marvel excellent.

VAIN IMAGININGS.

FROM all the jarring din of earth's low strife,
The hollow words, the vain false views of life ;
From petty rage, and eddying waves of care,
And multitudinous woes which rasp the air
With jangling discord ; from the waste of
    weeds
Where ill betides the growth of wholesome
    seeds ;
From love of self, disguised in Wisdom's garb
Where swift-tongued malice speeds her poi-
    soned barb,
I fled and sought a God who would me hear,
His poor low worshipper, in doubt and fear.

I stood upon the towering cliff
And looked upon the sea below :
" Art thou not great, O glorious sea,"
I said, " and powerful, and free ?
Speak in mine ear, or on the storm "—
But all the waters vast were still.

I looked into the blue of heaven
By day, and on the stars by night :—
" Art thou not high, thou vault of space ?
Ye stars, where is your resting-place ?
Tell me the height, the depth, O tell,
Seen and unseen, confess where dwell
The spirits of your hosts for ever ?
That silence never had been broken,
And silence made the words unspoken.

O Sun, O Source of Life and Light,
Art thou not to the angels bright ?
Shall death o'ertake thy hallowed beams,
And hail thee king, but king of dreams ?
Where shall thy glory bide and shine ?
Art thou delusion or divine ? "
No leaf, no blade around me stirred ;
No whispered hope my sorrow heard.

I sought the throne of the Supreme,
And prayed : " Thy works are as a dream—
Are they Thine own ?   They give no rest
To breaking heart and mind distrest ;
They live their life, if life it be,
But none hath aught to tell of Thee ;
And even we who all may scan
Know not the destiny of Man,
Nor why the worlds in circles roll,
Nor Him who guides and rules the whole.

We form our creeds and forge our prayers
But know not how our message fares.
Art Thou Creator, Father, God ?
O send not death before I hear ! "
If ever darkness reigned alone,
It reigned around me at His throne.

At length I rose, and said within myself
Mighty are words, and wisdom great indeed ;
But greater, greatest of all, is Patience.
And no seen power on earth prevaileth,
And patience in faith our task remaineth,
And duty doth well when worship faileth,
And afar, perhaps, the Unknown One reigneth

A star arose above my soul,
And joy and light glowed full and free.
I said : "O Love, I ask not thee
To grant what I did vainly seek,
For I am dumb, and thou dost speak ; "
And heaven and earth in chorus high
Returned one great harmonious cry :—
     " For ever."

AD SCIENTIAM.

Come with triumph songs about thee,
Noble, fair one, high descended,
Teacher of divine discoursings,
Angel of eternal truth !
Sister to religion holy,
Kindly in thine awful speech,
Stern and beautiful in virtue,
Mighty in reforming youth !

Horrid errors flee before thee,
Adoration steeped in sin,
Pious dreams in pomp dissolving,
Show of faith and void within ;
Flee the vanity of fables,
Flee the priesthood of the night,
Quench the taper shadow-raising,
Tell of universal light !
Pass away ye falsely holy,
Smotherers of Christian fire,
Preachers of a mute obedience
Damping down the golden lyre ;
Cast away your cunning palsied,

Shrouded in your killed conceit,
You have kept the world in darkness,
You shall drown in seas of light.
You have carved a paltry heaven
That your wretched key might serve,
Opening to the pence of sinners,
Closing to a martyr's prayers.
You have kept the world in darkness,
Coffined out the shining sky,
That your smoking torch might glimmer
Spectres to the blinded eye.
Millions tremble at the curses
Thundered in the name of Christ,
Pardons fill your choking purses,
Truly sin is precious grist !
Pomp in power sits approving
Sowers of the seed of shame,
Gospel truth is locked and guarded,
Churches' lies are swelled with fame.
So the past speaks, but the present
And the future loathe the tale,
We are risen to the hilltops
From the shadows of the vale.
Nevermore to wolfish traders,
Shall a nation's soul be bound ;
Goblin legends were for children,
Truth for men is right and sound.

Come then, Science, honour beaming
In thy bright and truthful eyes,

Step among the sordid peoples,
Raise them from their idols vile.
Maiden, cleave their rusted fetters,
Lead with many-sounding choir,
Bring them forth with hymning holy
Echoing to the starry sphere.
Teach them from the Book of Wisdom
Graven by no mortal hand,
Written from the ancient ages,
All may read and understand.
Living language burns before us,
Strong in everlasting type,
All who read may learn and worship,
Children of a larger life.
He that made the mind to reason
Must be greater than all thought,
He that formed the heart for loving
Must be greater than all love.
Give we then our souls high praises,
Truth in mind and love in heart,
These to regions blest will bear us
Ere the world's great war is past.

TWO FATES.

TENDER, and kind, and true,
Lovely, and sweet, and bright,
Dayspring that breaks from heaven,
To mortals seldom given,
Shedding a summer peace,
A joy that will not cease,—
>> Anguish to one.

Heart like the warm sun-streams
Of golden morning beams,
Wakening each soul to praise,
Shining through all our days,
Making the minutes a song
Of heroes for battle strong,—
>> A knell to one.

Turn not to see him grope,
Parted from health and hope,
By heaven and earth forgot,—
Thine is a better lot,
Crown of created life,
Noble as woman and wife,
>> God bless thy love.

THE KING.

WHO is the King? a man of men,
　A mind of nation-holding power
A hero, noble to maintain
　State-weal against an evil hour.

A warrior of the just and true,
　Quick to perceive his people's right,
Content with honour from the few,
　Slow to allow unworthy might.

Appealing ever from the heart
　To Him who sways eternal law,
And from the wisdom of the mart
　To higher wisdom's love and awe.

A friend compassionate and strong
　To brethren laid in suffering low ;
A scathing fire to rotten wrong,
　A light upon the path of woe.

A learner of the kindest thought,
　Of widest truth, of care humane,
That whatsoever things are taught
　May work for good in his domain.

Most gentle to the creatures meek
   Whose happy living is our trust,
Scorning because their cry is weak
   To lay their gladness in the dust.

Constructor in the social cause,
   Distilling strength from broad debate ;
Not recking much for swift applause,
   Or freshet floods of love and hate.

Severe in justice, not consenting
   To please a pity blind and small,
Nor slaying by undue relenting
   Where pain to few is peace to all.

Stern to reprove the subtler sin
   Which customs coax and judges pass,
The baleful pleasant things which win
   Corruption's way by fashion's glass.

Unsparing to the roots of ill,
   Subduing plagues to safe control,
Increasing joy and sure goodwill,
   A healer of the stricken soul.

So ruling that each mind may learn
   To rule himself in ordered ways,
That every shining light may turn
   Some fort of bad to heaven's praise.

Religious, reverent, and loyal
   To rubrics of the starry scroll,
Not suffering human craft to coil
   Vain incense clouds about the soul.

Awakener of war sublime,
   Explorer where none ever trod,
A glory to the coasts of time,
   A servant of the peace of God.

MILO'S ERRAND.

A LEGEND OF GREECE.

A STATELY lady dwelt in Macedon,
Whose name was Daphne, famed for flocks
      and herds,
But more for science and philosophy,
Deep knowledge of the stars and flowers and
      herbs,
And magic art to heal her ailing folk.
She learnt from Thales as her guide and guest,
For in old days oft sojourning awhile
For well-earned rest, the sage would freely
      talk
Oft in her presence of the things he loved.
Milo, her only son, dwelt with her ; him
The games most pleased and feats of giant
      strength,
Stalwart in body, but in mind a child ;
First prizeman in the great Olympic race.
Towered Irene was their dwelling-place,
About whose bulwarks stretched her emerald
      parks,
Renowned for horses trained for peace or 'war.

Then mighty men dwelt on the merry earth,
And sweet accord united State with State,
And all the isles rejoiced with songs of peace.
But years of mirth are oft repaid with grief,
And a great shadow stole o'er Grecian hearts
Like some dire ghost that haunts a festival,
For knowledge pierced the child-built walls of
    faith,
And truth of life in conscience was not sought,
And lacking righteousness a nation falls.
Empires loomed fateful in the West and East,
One to be dreaded for its giant strength,
The other for its autumn of decay.
In such a time lived Daphne and her son.

One morning, early, ere the faintest dawn
Blenched the bright radiance of the eastern
    stars
A messenger from Thales came in haste,
Bearing a note ; thereat she roused her son,
Saying the time had come whereof she dreamt,
And she must gird him for a mightier deed
Than on the world's stage had been done
    before.
He rose and broke his fast, and spoke no word,
Then, not too willing, stood before the gate,
Then spoke his mother, in less doubtful guise :
My son, the gods are gone to feast to-day
With the Ethiopians in their golden groves,
Leaving alone to guard the sacred fire

That glows for ever on Olympus' top,—
More subtle element than aught we know,
Whereby the jewels of the gods are wrought,—
Hephæstus, who is lame and runneth ill.
Lo ! Phœbus will forsake the heavens to-day,
This is the time for one who bides his time.
Ambition shrinks not before men or gods ;—
Thou art the fleetest runner of the Greeks.
Had'st thou not joy to wear the victor's crown,
And great delight to swoon in loud applause
And to be hailed incomparably first ?
Yet that is small renown and passing praise ;
I will that thou be famous for all time,
The man who gave the flame of gods to men.
Now therefore go, but use thy wariest sense,
And creep the flank of the great Mount with
        care,
For though the lame god sleep, his sleep is
        light,
And he has eyes more subtle far than thine,
And the least tremor of the earth, or flash
Of common fire, marring the pale light,
Will start him to his feet, and woe to him
On whom the hammer of Hephæstus falls.
Pass then the line of everlasting snow,
Mark how hè lies upon the marble hearth
High above storms, taking unwonted ease,
The brawny builder of those halls of Zeus
Set in the firmament's eternal blue,
Where never pain or mortal cares endure ;

And so approach that from behind his head
Swiftly this torch dipt in the deathless flame
Shall not appear nor move the light calm air.
Thou knowest now the mission of my love,—
Nobler is none wherein to live or die.
Then answer Milo made, inspired with zeal :
Thy word, O mother, is my soul's first law ;
I cannot doubt, since thou hast bid me go,
That this great errand has a pious end,
And, when the anger of the gods is past,
Will raise us mortals to be sons of Zeus.
If Hermes teach me, 'tis a worthy theft,
And the immortals ever love the bold.
I will bring back the secret fire of heaven,
And thou shalt love me better for the feat ;—
Till then look kindly on my lowlier zeal,
And guard the joy that crowned our simpler
    days.
Then, taking from her hand the torch, he sped
Across the plain, and ere the sun dissolved
The morning vapours in Thessalian dells,
Rested and drank at the Pierian spring
Near where sweet Tempe spreads her bounteous
    glades,
And gathered strength for his main enterprise ;
But prayed not to the gods, for it seemed best
To ponder praise-hymns for his safe return.
Thus mortals oft grow pious ere they sin.
So up the slope with joyful step he climbed
Through the large forest and thick underwood,

And rushy marshes and sweet thymy meads,
And over steep rock-knolls with wild-rose
    bright
And honey-heather banks and treeless tors,
Then long curved shoulders of small grass,
    where sheep
Scampered before him, and a cold wind blew ;
And then past patches of grey winter snow
Reached the fresh snow all crisp and sparkling
    white ;
Here his breath quickened and his temples
    ached,
And the blood tingled in his head and ears,
So he sought refuge from the cutting blast
Till his vext senses should o'ertake his feet.
An ice chasm lay upon his left, a cataract
Of tossing boulders and blue billows frozen,—
There in a clear ice-cave he found repose ;
But Zephyr or some other dæmon knew
Milo's intent, and gave him unsought sleep,
And day revolved and passed its middle
    height,
And Phœbus sprang from a dark sullen cloud,
And shot upon the mountain-side his beams,
Which darting fateful through a globe of ice
Anon with concentrated rays set fire
To Milo's torch dropped listless by his side ;
He, wakened by the smell, arose and stamped
His foot upon it, and the harm seemed slight,
Save a few tar-drops oozing from the end.

Angry, he scaled with rapid leap and run
The horrid crags hung round with icicles,
The deep snow-roofs, where he who pauses
    sinks,
The narrow ledges where a sloping inch
Hurls to a grave where all mankind might
    sleep
Buried in snow-drift, and the smooth white top
Above the wreathing clouds, shut out from
    earth,
Where the gods revel in perpetual light.
There in a climate of supreme content,
Compassed by palaces of glorious art,
In the mid-court that communed with the
    stars
Milo stood still in grave triumphant mood
Behind the forgeman of the gods ; a man
First of mankind to dare so proud a deed.
A change had come upon the face of heaven,
The sun above was darkened in eclipse.
His mother Daphne prayed for him at home :—
Ye influences of everlasting law
That mould unseen the fretful hours of life
Passed in the vale, unmindful of what awe
And holy beauty in the sphere of time
Prisoned awhile may lift our grovelling sense
To comprehend a source of all divine,
More lovely than the loveliest and the best,
Half felt, but crushed in our rough mortal
    grasp,—

Come to this son of earth, purge clear his view,
Make him your minister, a son of light,
Breaking the slow march of blind Nature's
    tread,
To bring new hopes with energy divine
Streaming from heaven upon the hearts of
    men.—
The flame shone pale and clear. Hephæstus
    slept,
Or seemed to sleep and live in pleasant
    dreams.
Milo leaned forward and no breath escaped,
Then touched the cincture of immortal light
But for a moment, and the strange glow hung
To mortal matter and he felt no shock,
Nor did the earth quake or the heavens fall,
For the blind gods made merry feast below.
Then turned he homewards leisurely and sang
A low-breathed song for pardon to great
    Zeus ;—
But scarce had moved a bowshot when a flash
Lurid and red gleamed for a moment round
From the blest dwelling-place, and Milo knew
That the pitch driven to the end had fallen
From his maimed torch into the changeless
    fire.
Forth strong Hephæstus strode with lifted
    mace,
Bellowing tremendous vengeance to the
    wrekin,

Then spied his little foe, and hobbling ran
And scored the rocks for splinters with his
    mace
Sent flying down, and loud the stone courts
    clanged
With fifty quoits, new-made to serve the gods,
Whizzed at his head ; but at the grassy slope
His lameness stopped him, and he cried in
    grief :
Beware thy fate, bring back that thunder fire !
I can forgive thee for thy reckless deed,
If now repented of, if hid from man ;
But if thou turn not back, the gods will know
Who stole their lightning, and thy place on
    earth
Shall hold thy ashes but thyself no more !
But Milo little recked, and in his mind,
Grown sage and ardent since he held the fire,
Saw the bright vision of a nobler race
And well-won gratitude and worthy joys,
With right intelligence of unseen truth
And high-souled music moving in the throng
Raised to a truer sense of light divine,
The passion of great hearts redeeming all ;
When not fast bound on one ethereal height,
But like free air and circumambient light
Reason might lift all voices in one song,
And love lead reason to her wider home.
But while he ran so fast and so elate
The torch's hot and deathless flame blew back

And he, all careless grown in his high state,
Heeded no smart, nor chid the sultry south
That drove the Libyan wind about his face,
Nor stayed again by the Pierian spring,
But hasted homewards lapped by lambent
    tongues
Of airy flamelets eating round and round,
And held aloft the omen of new life.
Yet neither he nor any eye beheld
The subtle element that struck his heart.
Now as he strove his blood ran cold and hot,
His knees grew weaker, and his spirit faint,
And he remembered a sharp fever caught
Swimming his toy-boat on the marsh, and
    vowed
He would not so succumb in sight of home.
And with strong will and care for every step,
Intent on that for which he went and came,
He reached Irene, and against the door
Fell with a faint cry.   The dry lintel smoked.
Forth came the lady Daphne and beheld
Enough to freeze her voice and stun her
    heart ;
She could not speak, but clasped his neck and
    wept ;
But all her tears could not allay his hurt,
For now, behold ! what his fierce duty
    spurned
To note—the arms, and breast, and face, half-
    charred

And scorched to blackness ;—but life still
    remained.
The torch lay gleaming in the garden roses,
Where he had set it, but none heeded now.
He raised himself to speak, she leant to hear,
Plying her remedies without avail.
She questioned, and he told her in weak words
That he was happy,—her behest was done,
And he had heard the music of the spheres.
Then a few sentences of parting sorrow
And passionate remorse and love from her
Closed the deep twilight as the stars came
    forth.
But when like very distant bells at evening
The tones of her he loved came from without,
The maiden who made earth so dear to him,
He raised himself once more, and for her sake
His voice fell gently like the dying pulse
Of the soft ripple of the summer sea,
That sinks to silence on the silver sand.
Then the wind rests and bright clouds turn to
    shades.
The wondrous fire for which his last words
    pleaded
A place in Science under Daphne's care
No search discovered.   Irene was a grave.
But rumours of the gods' tame lightning
    lingered
And never wholly passed from earth's dull
    shore,

And men half-hearted sought in their own
    way
To pierce towards truth of which they were
    too fearful,
As Milo was too eager, and they failed.
And not till years in thousands rolled away,
And wiser Science worked with mightier
    means
To gather service from deep-hiding Nature
By slow approaches of exalted minds
Till the whole earth was bound with nerves
    of thought
And human voices sped from town to town,
And light and motion sprang to finer form,
Could the full boon of Milo's hapless deed be
    known
Who stole electric flame from the Olympian
    throne.

FAIRYLAND.

THE FAIRIES' MORNING SONG.

Shake the dewdrops from the grasses,
Rain them on the thirsty ground,
Touch the cornflower and the daisy,
Thread the wheat between and round ;
Dip and paddle in the clover
While the pools lie on the leaf,
Wipe you dry with poppy petals
Shelter under violets take.
There the eastern light shall strike you
Flooding all with golden rays,
Hiding you like stars with brightness
From the bane of mortal gaze.
Through the thicket's elm and elder,
By the hawthorns to the glade,
Where the fern-stem curling upward
Breaks the brown peat in the shade,
And broad oaks with cooling leaf-cloud
Roof their curled and couching roots ;
On to where the bright-stemmed beeches,
Freshly dressed in silky green,
Chase the moss with softened sunshine

And the quick brook darts between.
Where the birch tree ever bonnie
Trusts her frailty to the sky,
Or the dark pine tosses upward
Sombre glory free and high ;
There the ground is dry and wholesome,
Fancy breathes her quickest air,
And the heavy gait of mortals
Doth not tread or linger there.
Heather buds and blooms around us,
Quarry for the storeful bee,
And the rocky knolls grow tender
Looped about with fair wild rose.
Wake ye, wake ye, drowsy bluebells,
Wake ye, daisies of the lawn,
Open out, ye river lilies,
Sweet anemones, unclose,
Woodland creatures, bright and ready,
Lift your eyes and drink the breeze,
Sun hath kept his evening promise,
Greet him from the topmost trees.
Starts the fawn from thick brake covert,
Sings the thrush her second song,
All the world goes forth to labour,
Plodding man has risen long.
Happy so to see the thronging
Multitude of creatures kind,
Happy so to hear the humming
Mill-wheel of creation blind.
We who live and laugh for ages

Turn their silly cares to jest,
In their noon of turmoil slumber,
All with us is fun or rest.
Toil is needless, money lumber,
Wealth is round us everywhere,
Why should anxious thoughts encumber
Sprites that live on sun and air ?

THE STATESMAN.

1877.

THERE stands a man among us whose great
    soul,
High aiming above mean and sordid things,
Ascends to reason, reaches forth to right,
Not for his own but for all human weal,
Not for a fame to win a shout and die,
Nor for a judgment in earth's current coin,
But in the eye of heaven doing battle
Unshaken in the midst of enemies,
Unblinded in the tumult and the storm,
Breaking the bonds of pride and links of lies,
Scorning to narrow down his star-wide view
And mix his arrows in the poisoned bowl ;
Rather he dips in the immortal stream
Of heaven-born light the winged words of his
    war,
And trusts that when he falls the glimmering
    dawn,
Which ever promises illumination more
To gladden the sad walk of human kind,
Will not decrease but brighten into day.

Then O that, when among the stony places
And desert tracks of life and burning ills
A prophet walks with valid arm and eye,
We may forsake our wisdom of the world,
Artful in carping as if tricks were life,
And moonshine prudences and creeping sneers;
O may we share with him some eminence
And hail him great as somewhat great our-
    selves!
In every age a saviour lifts his voice,
Him hearing well, a nation may be saved.

THOMAS CARLYLE.

Feb. 6, 1881.

GRIEVE not for him who leaves the world less
    poor—
He lived his life—nor let thy spirit mourn
The great soul free from all its earth-born
    woes,
The heart-springs blended with the sea of
    heaven.
There sinks the dust of day and all is clear.
Turn not away if words too rough have
    bruised ;
For oft an elf sits in a great man's heart
To pelt his would-be worshippers with clods,
Lest they enthrone Divinity in time
And close the boundless in a house of clay.
But learn him well, and follow him and love ;
Earth hath no living son more charged than he
With the cloud-piercing flashes of authority ;
And he is worthy of disciples true,
Not flatterers of words or images
Or foibles of the mighty dead, their master ;
But open minds, strong in the toil of thought,

Nobly performing in the faith of freedom
The will of ripest Reason. Let not Act
Lag short of Counsel, following slow with
 shame,
But give wise conscience scope, for he who
 spurns
That star-sure guide, fixed by eternal law,
Comes near the sin against the Holy Ghost.
So may our deeds forestall our words, and
 match
The faith of heroes, weighed, refined, and tried.
It hath been said of old, by One who spoke
With power, man cannot live by bread alone,
But by each word proceeding from his God.
Every right thought that burns in human
 hearts
Descends from heaven to be our sustenance ;
Therefore it is our part to hear and heed,
Not lightly wondering let the prophet pass.
He reared a rocky range of high-heaved thought
With faults and fissures, yet magnificent,
In peaks of granite splendidly forlorn,
Tossed with confusion towards the silent sky—
Far from their goal, yet a good span removed
From that low earth whose husk they burst in
 scorn
In the vast throb of some primeval woe.
That crag's world shock and thundering throes
 are gone ;
Its name is Silence, and the Waste of Wrath.

But in the clefts thereof grow tender herbs,
Tempering the harsh air with sweet graceful-
    ness,
Softening the restful slopes for weary limbs,
And breathing memories of old Eden's calm.
Green waving uplands too with breezes fresh
He finds for us, where clogging ills, toil-spun
Of Babylonian wisdom, wane and flee.
He gave a voice to that mute mystery
Of earth and heaven, Infinity and Man,
Which they who seek, not less than they who
    gaze,
Ponder with awe, mistrustful to translate ;
For words can but soar towards eternity
With temporal wings, soon faint, anon fall
    prone
Like birds beyond the clouds. The Sage did
    well
That with a giant's strength he flung the dross
Which from the glowing melting-pot of Science
O'erleapt and slid among the multitude—
Scrambling for signs and marvels—hurled it
    out,
And bid them rather seek for things not seen.
Yet known and knowing are but parts of one
Eternal thought ; both night and day are
    blessed ;
Science is greater than he knew or taught.
As on a parching land the west wind lights,
Shower-laden, from the ever-heaving sea,

Dispels the withering blight of dewless days,
While through the woods a joyful chorus
    breaks
From leafy branches stretching to the breeze ;
Apace the watery boon in plashy gusts
Washes despondency from men's weak hearts,
So for no paltry end his blast went forth,
Rushing unbidden through the haunts of care.
Like the storm-sough of some majestic pine
When all is still below, we heard it pass,
And knew the sultry plague of drought was
    stayed,
The russet mead would spring in sweeter crop,
The failing wells of nations flow fresh-filled.
Deep, deep, thy woe, unutterably deep,
O man, and as thine eye hath pierced
The immeasurable heavens more and more,
So hath thy sorrow grown divinely strong,
And the whole heart is faint and tossed in
    doubt,
And the small lights of the dark vault immense
Wax dim, and lo ! the vile hard earth beneath,
Willing to nourish the mere beast of Nature,
Disowns the child that 'fines its common dust
Beyond the quest of gross necessities,
Seeking for angels among blank gaunt tombs,
With spirits high communion holding, rapt
In ecstasies of heaven, resolved, inspired,
Supremely strong for war. Poor toy of dreams !
The eagle lifted thee to swell thy joy

In the white sunlight, and to view the array
Of hosts to conquer ; in the next black hour,
Crawling and groping among broken bones
Through the wide charnel-house of ancient
    cares,
Slowly thou mendest sinews of bruised thought,
Coping with inward phantoms of despair,
Sore-stricken even when men's cup runs over,
In vintage and in harvest quite cast down.
But thy sad lot shall not endure for ever
And Hope and Faith, whose shattered temples
    moan,
With murmuring echoes, shall return with
    power,
The life of life in all, the quenchless Lamp,
The heavenly kingdom which makes all truth
    one,
Whose high and holy influence is Love.
Therein no thing unworthy can take root ;
And in this wondrous era, when the deep
Reveals its fountains, and the astonished eye
Must gaze or close her lid in blind alarm,
To us who have the strength of battled years,
Hope bears a glorious increase ; from the vale
Of dark past ages travel-worn emerged,
We edge the dawn-illuminated brow
Of a new world, regenerate, free-born,
Rejoicing in the yet far-off Humanity
Towards which the Spirit of All Good doth
    work.

Thus forward on our path ! The sun above
Is but a traveller, and the stars as sparks
Tell forth the rays of an unreckoned fire,
In which all light shall centre. It is well.
Earthquake and storm spake not. But in the
    calm
The heaven-wide voice, the Everlasting Yea.

GIORDANO BRUNO IN PRISON
BEFORE HIS MARTYRDOM BY FIRE.
Feb. 6, 1600.

O Wondrous All, O God through all supreme !
O Infinite, through Thee both strong and wide !
Space filled with Life, all living sprung from
    Love,
Working through darkness to the illuminate
    sea :
O Universe of Being, starry choir,
Ever aspiring in sublime array,
Hymning the Holder of your spacious dome :
Flame-hidden glory ever near and far,
Untiring Reason, will of sovereign good,
High throne where truth's immortal fountain
    springs :
O Primal Brightness whose felt word is Light,
O form and multitude, O gallery vast
Of heavenly beauty, shadowed glass of Law,
That mighty impress of the mind of God,
Divine reflection of diviner thought :
All bodied systems, breathing worlds and shapes
Telling of Him the maker without end !

One Truth, one Goodness, fills and governs
    all,
Heaven moves our will, the voice of ages
    speaks—
The Soul of souls is unity undying,
Essence of being, cause and spring of right,
Substance immutable, to sense obscure,
To reason visible, the bond of time,
Ethereal Infinite, uniting grace,
All members of one vast harmonious whole,
Immortal power of stars and souls and things.
O human image, spirit clothed in flesh,
Earth animate, by tender longing swayed,
Sky-cleaving sunbeam, child of the All-wise,
With wonder rapt, and reverence ever young :
O beating consonance and passion high,
Thrilling and melting through the song of
    death,
In least and greatest omnipresent good,
Kind breadth and depth and volume of de
    light—
Be with me now, spirit of humankind,
Souls of all saints and blessed pure in heart
Burn out each baseness with your holy fire.
Comfort my loneliness, inspire my night,
Refresh my memory with the dews of dawn,
And clear my conscience for the perfect day.
    Thou who informest for the last great change,
    I live and move and keep my soul in Thee,
    Therefore I fear not as the guilty may,

Thy truth is peace, Thy bidding my loved
　　care,
I build my prison with Thy mysteries.
I perish by a faithfulness despised,
Not comprehended here, yet in full time,
When smoking mountains are extinct on
　　earth,
And spiritual kings are throned on love,
Some wanderers may revisit the scorned cell,
And gather stones to found the Church of
　　Man.
Come, gentle Guide to everlasting day,
Lift me, not sadly, children of the blest,
From this dim spot ; receive, diviner air,
This too rebellious citizen of earth,
Him who in awe beheld, who fiercely fought,
Too eager for the truth which cannot die,
To spread her glory over land and sea.
I pass, but thou shalt live, O Truth,
With grace and beauty in the hearts of men.
O sweet defeat, and dear forgiven world,
My heart bleeds only for your blind offence,
Your wrong will touch and hurt me, not these
　　flames,
May every pang that shoots my body through
Redeem some captive, break some prison bar,
Make bold some lone one, some oppressor just,
And wake more widely than this dying voice
Some new celestial music on the earth.

PROCLAIMING THE PAPAL SEN-
TENCE AGAINST LUTHER.
MAY 12, 1521.

A DAY of solemn pomp and holy zeal.
In the full dignity of Church and State
My Lord the Cardinal Archbishop comes,
Legate of Rome, Commissioner of Heaven,
With royal honours, to proclaim a curse,
The blasting thunder of the Vatican.
The bishops of the realm, beneath St. Paul's,
The Dean and Doctors, and high officers,
And noble prelates, meet him nigh the dome,
Praising with humble voices his proud reve-
    rence
And mighty power for the glory of God,
Whereby his enemies will flee like chaff.

Incense goes up, my lord is on his way
To the high altar, all the people bow
As slowly up the nave he passes more than
    king,
Under a canopy of cloth of gold
Borne by four doctors ; then, his service done
Forth to the Cross in Paul's Churchyard he
    moves.

RESPICE.

As years roll on with ever-hastening speed,
And life contracts, and ever sharper need
Our spirits feel, aghast 'mid woe and crime
Of some bright gleams to cheer the stormier
    clime,
When toil seems vain, and hope a failing
    light,
And fate, world-ruling, blasts the seeds of
    right,—
Where shall I voyage for the faith I lack?
Dark looms the future—Memory breathes
    " Look back ! "
In scorn I turn, fooled wise with honoured
    lies,
But lo! heaven's grace bedews my tortured
    eyes ;
Athwart the thundergloom that frowns be-
    tween
The hallowed heights of youth shine fair and
    green,
A sunlit islet high above the storm,
Where flowers grew wild which learning can-
    not form ;

There, at the touch of an Immortal Will
The clear soul woke, resolved, sublime, and
     still ;
So kind, so lovely, were the days gone by ?
Since this hath been, I've strength to live and
     die.

IMPATIENCE.

PRESUMPTUOUS, eager, shallow fool of Now
To probe Hereafter ; should I say by night,
Like some scared babe—"The morn will never
    come,"
Or doubt that winter will give place to spring,
Or wars to peace, folly to Reason's ray ?
Who knows the burden of the tide of time,
Or whether Time himself may not find death
Within himself, no potentate in heaven ?
We are but measurers of the measureless,
The oceans of the Soul are unexplored,
Our limits and our logic fade and fall
In the wide radiance that fills angel's eyes.

As feathery sunset clouds, sublime and bright,
Did battle once within the stormy deep
Till the great Sun, compassionate and kind,
Looked forth upon their lawless, dark dis-
        tress,
And where the angry waters met in foam
Gathered some weary atoms from that strife
To glow in glorious peace amid the blue,
So stand the Incorruptible on high
And render music from unnumbered spheres.

VOICES.

I.

BEAM forth, O God, upon this darkened world,
Make each true martyr draw men's hearts to
 Thee,
Give resolution to our wavering ranks
And courage to endure earth's sharpest woes,
Maintain good hope when fear and death are
 strong,
And love toward Thee when surging hate
 assails,
Bind us in faith when shadows dark and grim
Cast their weird images on weeping eyes,
And sweet remembrance shines but in a
 dream,
And Truth enfolds herself in shrouds of
 gloom ;—
Come to us then, and if some vast despair
Floods like an ocean round our shattered
 home,
Let firmest duty, knowing right alone,
Steer us through midnight to thy perfect
 peace.

II.

Not time, or aught that on time's law depends
Can heal the wounds of every broken heart,
Not wisest counsel or the voice of friends
Can heal death's ravage, or give joy for smart ;
Yet from the deep of sadness there may spring
Duty's calm conscience and glad suffering :
Betwixt surrender of the soul's high walk,
Treason to right, fierce welcome to despair,
And perfect nobleness, love's own new life,
There lies no middle land,—the world is
    naught
But the vexed bank which heaven's bright
    fountains cross,
They have their being otherwhere than here :
Thence flows immortal strength, and all that
    seems
Is but Eternity's sad waking dreams.

III.

Most true, most dear, most tender, and most
    bright,
Daughter of joy against all sorrow shining,
In earth's dark sky thou wast my star of light,
Thou shalt be strong to quell my heart's re-
    pining;
High resolution on thy brow did rest,
Courage and scorn for life's poor mocking
    show,
No common idols swayed thy noble breast,
God loved thy hope, and God sustained thy
    woe.
As down the vale, robbed of my whole delight
I journey, wondering at thy shortened day,
All things of time, and dreams of sense and
    sight
Dissolve like mist beneath the morning ray :
Since for eternity one perfect life
Showed forth one love in one perfected
    thought,
Since God spake clear, what need of doubt
    and strife ?
The heart of heaven makes man's anguish
    nought.

IV.

Bright soul ! sweet flower of all beauteous
    thought,
Religion's image, radiant child of love,
All good and true and tender work is thine,
A melody of grace, a hymn of joy,
To lighten heavy hearts, make doubt ashamed,
And thrill our being with resounding praise.
Mortal immortal, masterpiece of time,
Why treadest thou this changing isle of dust,
Thyself soon perishing from this poor stage
Into the night ? from God thou surely camest ;
Substance made moving could not flash from
    blindness
So pure a shrine, nor chaos build that heart.

  Constraining power, blest hope of a dark
     world,
  Angel of peace, heaven's gleam in the
     storm's rack,
  Even the wrongdoer hears an answering
     voice
  Within him, worshipping as thou goest by,—
  God keep one ever such as thee on earth !
  More true than truth, than paradise more
     fair,
  To have known thee is to subdue despair.

V.

Blest soul of heaven's eternal truth of good,
Dear noble presence of inspiring love,
In thy clear light the path of mortal care
Lay straight and plain through danger and
    distress,
With pain our friend and death our fixed
    adieu,
To that fair region where all partings cease
And faithful hearts fulfil the task of God :
Thy voice so tender bore an angel's song,
Thy glorious smile made earth too near to
    heaven ;
If in full joyance thou hadst not passed forth
Days had been worshipped and thy home
    divine ;
But since thou art not here, all seen is strange,
Life hath no ease, corruption no despair,
I long to breathe but in immortal air.

VI.

TO A PATRIOT.

Right on ! though blocked in every forward
    path,
Right on ! though Fate breeds horrors day by
    day,
And serpents cling to thee from Stygian pools
Stirred in their murderous mud by thy fierce
    light,—
Keep still thy heart, and raise thy trumpet
    blast
Untrembling clear above the crackling thorns
And legioned follies which tease meagre souls,
With callous counsellors whose creed is dust ;—
Thy lightning stroke has torn the chains of
    hate,
Which turn glad life into a slavish march,—
Thy pity shineth under every star,
And suns unrisen shall beam on fairer fields,
Blessing thy manhood that in timorous days
Bore hope unblinded to the gates of hell.

VII.

Why toil, if labour be not means of good ?
Why rest, if day draw not its hope from
    dark ?
Why live, if life be not a conquering march,
Or breathe, if breathing may no creature
    bless ?
Our strength is faith, our reverence is worth,
And in obedience man fulfils his law ;
Erring is dying, ignorance disease,
And feeble counsel saps a nation's heart,
Man has to know, the stars in order run,
Unconscious right rebukes fore-reasoned
    wrong ;
Forget old self, new self is human weal ;
If wisdom circulates and right hath limbs,
Blood finds the heart, and age finds peace in
    life,
There is no loss but loss of hope and love,
And bodies dying bid more loving live.

VIII.

If nature, smitten with too late remorse,
Creating hearts that feed their love for loss,
Should turn and bring the lords of conscious
    life
To feel no memory and forecast no pain,
Born, growing, dying in half-happy trance,
No more in wild lament beholding death
That crowds all nobleness to silent graves,
No more uplifting sense and prayer and work
To one high mind that never did respond,—
Then what should one spared from the kind
    decline
And looking boldly on that vast release
Say in himself, the last of suffering souls ?
God, if thou livest, bring back those children
    lost,
Make them in agony at one with Thee !

IX.

Seek not thy God in wonders or in signs,
Or through the service of an empty heart ;
He is not man who to mere words inclines
Or conjures faith with any sudden art ;
He is no king to deal rewards or pains,
Or stranger to be pleased with rare regard ;
He loves not jewelled shrines or pillared fanes
Where pride of sense the humble prayer hath
        marred ;
His marvels live in every place and hour,
Through every moment countless wonders
        shine,
He changeth not though man may smile or
        lower,
But every creature moves in the divine.
Not in the showy pomp of outward things
Our spirits rest—Truth hides from careless
        eyes—
Nor yet from heights where reason plies her
        wings
Behold full wisely the unmeasured skies.
Barren the icy calm of hard-won peaks,
Struck by all sunshine, but retaining none,
Better to grieve where woe to sorrow speaks
In the dark city, than exult alone.

Seek then thy God in all the good He
    gives—
He hides His leaven in the hearts of men,
He striveth ever against ill, and lives
Thy nearest friend,—thy soul is born again.

X.

Guard well thy steps beyond the beaten
    way,
For many dangers compass venturous turns ;
If thou hast left the credulous crowd behind,
Make not credulity thy guide abroad ;
Better the known deceit, where thou art true,
Than truthful things with thee their false
    high priest ;
Better the myth of mirage than of mine,
The day-born phantom than the earth-born
    flame,
The doubtful dogma than the new-hatched
    sign,
Wisdom begins where knowledge finds her
    goal.
    Noble to spurn the dross of crabbed creeds,
    More noble still to weld the white-hot truth
    Into bridge girders crossing bog and stream,
    Firm as a rock above the wilds of doubt,
    A way for armies to the promised land.

XI.

Where is the path of ever-hallowed joy,
The life worth living and our true content ?
Not in the thronging vanities of crowds,
The credit of convention, dull and dense,
The show of wit, or press for short applause,
Or heavy sports, and skill devoid of sense.
No bloody pastime can be God's high call
To reasoning spirits, or the end of life,—
If soul be in us, soul must break the wall
Of creature custom, and command the strife.
Fair nature under reason must have sway,
The breezy fields to brooding thought give
    health,
Our orbit still must her good laws obey,
Her pastures profit more than choking wealth.
Rule is most honoured which most freedom
    gives,
And within rule all worthy freedom lives.

XII.

He who through temperate and mastered life
With single eye his chosen work performs,
Swerves not to right or left, but strong in
    will
Rides through the blasts which weaker craft
    may sink,
Though little to the world in talk or fame,
Conquers more nobly than that Cæsar Gaul,
Who reared an empire by the strokes of
    force,
With blood cemented, and in blood ere long
With dire disruption broken and dissolved,—
For virtue strengthens with each conquest
    won,
And the foe passions, after years of war
Subdued, rise never to dislodge their lord ;
God gives the increase, power comes un-
    sought,
And light celestial crowns that soldier's
    brow,
So fate may thwart and rankling evils rise,
He stands their match and still victorious
    dies.

XIII.

Come, hallowed Spirit of the souls of men,
Sustain the heart that hath no help but Thee,
Dissolve these thronging troops of bitter cares
That sting and harry us to abject graves,
Be with us in all deeds and bless each thought,
Make every duty be a task from Thee ;
Thy kingdom come, Thy will be done on
    earth,—
Thy will is good, O let the good be done
On earth as ever it is done in heaven,
The full joy of the life of perfect souls
The harmony of comprehending Thee.
O burn the blight thou hatest from the world,
Lift the thick darkness that breeds plagues
    and crimes
And save, O save, the souls that trust in
    Thee.

XIV.

O Mystery, mute Spirit of the world,
Breathing through all, silent amid all voices,
Silent and strong, unseen however sought,
Life of all being, moving among Thy blind,
Blind matter, blind animal, blind souls of men,
O Thou, not he whom in a thousand shapes
Men worship and call God, but One not far,
Whose spirit loves the loving, and doth come
Softly each moment to thy children's cry
And fightest evil through the toils and cares
Of struggling creatures towards some distant
    dawn,—
Source of all Right and Light, in this vexed
    nook
Of mis-creation, justified unfaith,
Maimed bodies and minds warped with sore
    distress,
If thou art mighty, make thy goodness strong,
That we uncrushed may love thee perfectly
With heart and soul, nor need these mills of
    pain,
Nor human wrecks to mark the path of
    wrong.

XV.

Spirit who dwellest where all wisdom dwells,
In light eternal centering all life,
Shed Thy pure strength upon our mortal
    ranks,
That when we lift our eyes in trembling hope
Faith may transform us from low penitence
To songs of gladness, confident and free,
That while we labour at appointed work,
All hours may pass in communing with Thee.
Learning Thy wisdom that shall change all ill
And bring even Fate a captive to Thy law,
Then grant us plenitude of love and zeal
Strong constant virtue, which alone becomes
Man in thy image ; so embracing sleep,
In the last day our souls shall wake unbound.

WESTMINSTER ABBEY.

OCT. 15, 1892.

CALL him not dead whose life is in the ages,
Whose body bindeth him to earth no more,
Dust joineth dust, but through ascending
    stages,
Soul maketh voyage to the unseen shore.

Give *him* not burial, give earth to earth,
That form which God most wondrously en-
    dowed,
There leave it tranquil, even from his birth
He far transcended shapen sun and cloud.

If heaven hold him, sing no dirges here,
Thy clinging thought is nearer tombs than he,
Mountains of stones would cover but a bier,—
Spread broad thy sail upon the boundless sea.

Thy life is free ; thou canst increase his glory,
Build him a monument in truth and deed,
Thou canst make nobler the great human
    story,
Live his best melody,—the world hath need.

BEFORE SUNRISE.

THE dawn's tide flows, the pale moon wanes
    and sinks
Before the splendour of our earth's great lord,
Appointed ruler of our little lives,
And all the motions of his planet sons,
Dispenser of light, warmth, and living force
According to the will of the Supreme,
Most high, who dwells in all and nourishes
All good through time to some celestial end.
We wot not, hemmed in by the savage brake
And underwood of ancient wilderness,
And clouded in by frequent dismal mists,
Whither we tend, but ever and anon
The music of a higher being wakes
And bears us speechless to Olympian courts
Whence soon we pass and fall. Within our
    hearts,
I doubt not, is a sun as great, as bright,
And brighter far to him who clears his gaze
And sees the sky-glow through the breaking
    crust
Of the dark mines wherein man's soul hath
    toiled
And struggles upward resolute through pain,
Till that immortal sun proclaims new birth
With more than life and more than temporal
    light.
If this I doubted, I were dead indeed.

8

TRANSLATIONS.

SONNET 44.   EROICI FURORI.—Giordano Bruno.

Such high desires cannot remove the veil
From this vexed mind, on holy splendour
    bent ;
The heart, which thought would fain create
    anew,
The heart, which vainly seeks one hour of
    ease,
Finds no retreat, but tossed from wave to
    wave,
Misses the loveliness of sweet repose.
These eyes which should be closed in softest
    sleep
Are all night open with complaint and grief.
What care and art will soothe my senses worn?
What balm bring solace to my straining
    sight ?
O Spirit, tell, what time or place can heal
Thy bitter groaning and thy pain intense ?
And thou, my heart, for sufferings so deep
Where can I find the offering of peace?
Where will the soul give you the tribute due,
O pain-wrought mind, O eyes and heart of
    woe ?

NÄHE DES GELIEBTEN.—GOETHE.

(Music by F. Schubert.)

I THINK of thee when rays of sunny gladness
    From ocean stream ;
I think of thee when deep in wells of sadness
    The moon doth gleam.
Thou art not lost when o'er the distant high-
    way
    The storm-cloud lowers ; ·
In darkest night when on the rocky byway
    The wanderer cowers ;
I hear thee still when loud with hollow
    thunder
    The billow breaks ;
When listening oft amid the silent forest
    Thy music wakes.
Though sundered far, I live without repining,
    Sure thou art near,
The sun goes down ; behold, the stars are
    shining ;—
    Would thou wert here !

AN DIE MUSIK.—Schober.

(Music by F. Schubert.)

"DU HOLDE KUNST."

Thou sacred Art, how oft in dreary moments,
When life's wild waves in gray confusion
    break,
Hast thou my heart with warmest love en-
    kindled,
And in thy peace hast bid a higher being
    wake,
      Hast bid a higher being wake.

Oft from thy lyre an air hath flowed appealing
With sweet and holy harmony to me,
A blessed heaven of better days revealing
Thou Art divine, my loving thanks to thee,
      Thou art divine, all thanks to thee.

"ANFANGS WOLLT' ICH FAST VERZAGEN."—
H. HEINE.

(Music by R. Schumann.)

When it came, I fell despairing
  Blind and burdened, bent and low,
And it seemed beyond my bearing,
  Yet I bore it—ask not how !

STILLE THRÄNEN.—J. KERNER.

(Music by R. Schumann.)

FROM sleep untroubled risen,
  Through flowers thy footsteps fall,
Beholdest radiant heaven
  Spread glory over all.

While thou in peace wast sleeping
  From pain and sorrow free,
Heaven all night long was weeping
  Its tears unknown to thee.

Hearts have their still dark sorrow
  Eyes rain unseen in woe,
But on the shining morrow
  Fair smiles are all ye know

"DU BIST WIE EINE BLUME."
—H. HEINE.

(Music by R. Schumann.)

THOU art a flower's image
　　So holy, pure, and kind,
Thy tenderness beholding
　　Love hallows all my mind.

It seems as though a blessing
　　Arose and filled my heart,
A prayer that God possessing,
　　Would keep thee as thou art.

"WILLST DU DEIN HERZ MIR GEBEN."

(*Quoted by Beethoven.*)

O wilt thou give thine heart ?
　Then let the token be
That none shall bear a part
　In thoughts I share with thee.
Let love that makes us blest,
　Reign deep in soul and will,
Let greatest joys and best
　Be hidden, calm, and still.

IHRE STIMME.—Graf von Platen.

(Music by R. Schumann.)

"LASS TIEF IN DIR MICH LESEN."

O READ me the deep wonder,
    The magic of thy voice,
O keep not ever under
    The current of its joys.

So many words keep thronging
    All empty to the ear,
And while we listen longing
    They vanish into air.

Yet far away thou speakest
    As when thou present art,
Thy tone when sounding weakest,
    Is mighty in my heart.

So kindled, so appealing,
    My spirit glows within ;
Thy voice and all my feeling
    Are too divinely kin.

HEIDEN RÖSLEIN.—Goethe.

(Music by Fr. Schubert.)

BAIRNIE spied a rosebud blow,
　Rosebud on the fair lea,
Fresh and bright as morning glow,
Quick he ran its grace to know,
　And it pleased him rarely.
　　　Rosebud, rosebud, rosebud red,
　　　Rosebud on the fair lea.

Bairnie cried, " I'll break thee off,
　Blooming on the fair lea!"
Rose made answer : " Then I prick,
And thou'll not forget me quick,
　Therefore touch me warily."
　　　Rosebud, rosebud, rosebud red,
　　　Blooming on the fair lea.

But the boy so rude and rough
　Plucked the rose unheeding,
Rose turned round and stang enough,
Ache and grief were vain rebuff,
　Nought availed her pleading.
　　　Rosebud, rosebud, rosebud red,
　　　Blooming on the fair lea.

"DU MEINE SEELE, DU MEIN HERZ."

(*Words by Fr. Rückert.   Music by R. Schumann.*)

"WIDMUNG."

To thee my soul, to thee my heart,
My pain, my prayer, my nobler part,
To thee my spirit's heaven and light
I lift and lose the cares of night :—
My firmament in which I move
To glow for ever in thy love !

O thou art rest, O thou art peace,
Blest spring wherein my troubles cease ;
O Love, thou mak'st me king from thrall,
In thee I reign and live for all ;
Thy glance doth give me power unknown,
And raise me wondering to thy throne.

My heart, my truth, for whom I sigh,
My law supreme, for ever nigh,
Thou life in which, no longer low,
My heaven of love, I move and glow,
Thou soul of good, my worthier Self.

THE SONG OF NORNA.

("GESANG DER NORNA."—SCHUBERT.)

My path is lone, and dark my way
   O'er gulf and stream and ocean deep,
The wild waves know my Runic lay,
   Fall glassy smooth and cease to leap.

The wild waves know my Runic lay,
   The seas are smooth, the torrent still,
But heart of man in storm and fray
   Scarce knows its own beclouded will.

One hour is mine in all the year
   To range with wail and moan the deep ;
'Tis then I rise with beacon clear,
   That flame dies down, I fall to sleep.

The beacon burns : 'tis dead of night :
   Hail ! Magnus daughters ; hear, O hear !
For you my wondrous tale is dight !
   Awake, arise ! O turn and hear !

ORISONS AND HYMNS.

RICHES.

CHRIST is come to ask thy life,
　Bring Him all thou hast and art ;
Earth can spare her treasures well,
　Heaven cannot spare thy heart.

Rest in God thy mind and will,
　Break the load of cares away,
Breathe the air of perfect faith,
　Let thy strength be as the day.

SURGAMUS.

CHRISTIAN ! rise, and act thy creed,
Let thy prayer be in thy deed.
Seek the right, perform the true ;
Thou canst make thy life anew.

Hearts around thee sink with care,
Thou canst help their load to bear,
Thou canst bring inspiring light,
Arm their faltering wills to fight.

Wrong shall die in open day,
Virtue shines beyond decay,
Falsehood flees from candour's face,
Health reflects eternal grace.

Principalities and powers
Still beset thy weaker hours.
Give them battle, seal their doom,
Angel-guests shall fill their room.

Let thine alms be hope and joy,
And thy worship God's employ ;
Give Him thanks in humble zeal,
Learning all His will to feel.

Come then, Law divine, and reign,
Freest faith assailed in vain,
Perfect love bereft of fear,
Born in heaven and radiant here.

ΟΥΡΑΝΟΣ.

God's lamps are stars and suns,
　　Their light is freely given,
And when their work is done,
　　That light returns to heaven.

God's field is on the earth,
　　He maketh fruits increase,
And from its very birth
　　Prepared it for our lease.

God's angels are with men,
　　And win them to His side ;
Their souls return again
　　When we say, " They have died ! "

And every work and thought
　　In life which marked the soul
To Him in truth is brought,
　　That He may make it whole.

———

Child ! though darkness close thee round
　　So that scarce thou drawest breath,
And the pleasant world is drowned,
　　And thou touchest only death,

Know, that if thy spirit bear
Through the long cold night of pain,
Thou shalt rise beyond despair,
And thy life shall not be vain.

WILL of our Father, infinite radiance,
Power of the Holiest, clear our dim sight,
Spirit of love, descending from heaven,
Bind us as brethren, and lead us to light.

O GOD, whose voice the angels hear,
Whose music beats through worlds un-
known,
Inform our hearts with power divine,
And raise pale doubt thy name to own.

Pour forth on us thy vital will,
Make plain the clouded coasts of heaven,
Bless all the people bowed in gloom
With kindled hope and burning zeal.

O Thou whose ocean's tide hath filled
Creation's space with kindly sway !
Touch every home, from shore to shore,
With gentle truth's immortal ray.

O Thou who guardest great and small,
Whose children own Thee Love Sublime !
Make strong each heart that on Thee waits,
Break down the pictured screen of time.

O Thou whose paths are sown with stars,
  Whose patience tendeth every child,
We thank thy love for life supreme,
  We praise for matchless hope thy word.

The daily toil, the flowery field,
  Shall concord sound and rapture breathe
The hosts of darkness prostrate fallen
  Shall rise redeemed to greet the morn.

O Thou whose reign the ages crave,
  Whose light unseen inspheres us all,
We lift, to join the choir on high,
  Our hearts' weak praise on wings of song.

Be Thou about us all our years,
  May all good works through Thee increase,
Let sweetest calm ensue from tears,
  From earth's brief war Thy perfect peace.

Come, Holy Spirit, kind to all,
  Arise on hearts where pride is slain,
Inspire the weak with passion high,
  And break in light o'er seas of pain.

Thou wilt have mercy, that I know ;
  I dare not ask Thy special care,
But lift my soul to thy good Power,
  And melt in tears my wordless prayer.

The least of earth who turns to Thee
  Is child beloved in angels' view ;
The present Soul of Life, unseen,
  Brings gifts of grace and joy most true.

I know Thee still, the Source of might,
  I crave Thee still, the perfect Love ;
Not any wandering far from right
  Can make heaven's blessèd law remove.

In Thee, O Soul of every good,
  Of highest beauty, truth revealed,
We live and move, and pierce the veil
  To glory's bright and boundless field.

COME unto me, ye weary,
  And I will give you rest ;
Come unto me, ye wounded,
  For they that mourn are blest.

Come unto me, ye prisoners,
  And heaven shall be your room ;
Come unto me, ye hated,
  For I have known your gloom.

Come unto me, ye laden,
  My love exceeds your days ;
Come unto me, ye wanderers,
  My tears are on your ways.

Come unto me, ye hungry,
  The Bread of Life is near ;
Come, all ye parched and thirsty,
  The spring of health is here.

Come unto me, ye children,
  Your angels ever there
In heaven behold our Father,
  And ye are each His care.

Come unto me, ye righteous ;
  In might rejoice, ye strong ;
Let music blend with brightness,
  And light abide in song.

Not as the world, I give you
  A wealth that all may spend,
A joy that never faileth,
  A treasure without end.

The grace of God be with you ;
  Your faith shall mountains move.
And yet unconquered regions
  Shall own the reign of love.

BREAK through the earth, arise in grace,
  Spread forth thy leaves to drink the light ;
May tender airs make sweet and strong
  Thy flower and branch, O Tree of Life !

The sky above, the ground beneath,
  Shall bear thee all their streams of good ;
Thy root shall hold, while high and higher
  Thy noble growth exalts the vale.

The bloom of faith, the fruit of power,
  Shall fill our hearts with peace sublime,
Thy glorious dome's imbowered choir
  Shall haven listening grief in song.

The gathering nations, armed for right,
  Shall counsel take beneath thy shade,
And heavenward anthems, hymns of love,
  Lift every human soul in praise.

THE Church of Christ ariseth
In silent beauty strong ;
Old jostling falsehoods, crumbling,
Disclose the plan of God.

The Church of Christ is lovely,
And blesseth every soul ;
Her only law is goodness,
Her only hatred sin.

The Church of Christ is friendship
To every earnest heart ;
Obedience, work, and healing
True mind and conscience clear.

The Church of Christ is reigning,
Of God in lives of men ;
Best thought and highest reason,
Love conquering ill and pain.

The Church of Christ is moving
From shadow into light,
From desert into pasture,
From weakness into might.

The Church of Christ is freedom
And reverential peace,
An evergrowing kingdom,
A Will that cannot cease ;

A glory born of saving,
Like suns that warm the worlds,
A fountain-spring of ardour,
A living grace for all ;

A treasure borne to heaven
By sighs too deep for words,
A strong and kind communion,
And deeds whose soul is prayer.

The Church shall live in candour
And temperance and praise ;
And ever-hopeful patience
And joy shall bless her ways.

Her gates shall open widely
To every child of man ;
And every earnest seeker
Shall make the Church of God.

www.ingramcontent.com/pod-product-compliance
Lightning Source LLC
Chambersburg PA
CBHW020752020726
47495CB00008B/2398